A Junior Novelization

Adapted by Daniela Burr
Based on the original screenplay by Elise Allen

SCHOLASTIC INC.

New York   Toronto   London   Auckland   Sydney
Mexico City   New Delhi   Hong Kong   Buenos Aires

ISBN 0-439-85636-1

BARBIE, FAIRYTOPIA, MERMAIDIA and associated trademarks and trade dress are owned by, and used under license from Mattel, Inc. © 2005 Mattel, Inc. All Rights Reserved.

Special thanks to Rob Hudnut, Tiffany J. Shuttleworth, Vicki Jaeger, Monica Okazaki, Mainframe Entertainment, Luke Carroll, Mike Douglas, Dave Gagnon, Derek Goodfellow, Teresa Johnston, Anita Lee, Sean Newton, Kelly Shin, Julia Ferguson, Byron Leboe, and Walter P. Martishius.

Published by Scholastic Inc.
SCHOLASTIC and associated logos are trademarks and/or registered trademarks of Scholastic Inc.

12 11 10 9 8 7   7 8 9 10/0

Printed in the U.S.A.
First printing, February 2006

Chapter 1
A Friend in Need

"Beat you!" Elina called out excitedly as she zipped past her friend Dandelion. She smiled triumphantly. After all, she'd won a race . . . a *flying* race. That was quite new to her.

For a long time, Elina had been the only fairy in all of Fairytopia who could not fly. She'd traveled on the ground while the others flew. But now she, too, had her wings. And the feeling of flight was absolutely incredible.

Fairytopia was a magical place, watched over by the wise Enchantress. It was the Enchantress herself who had given Elina wings, as a reward for the courage she'd shown by saving Fairytopia from the evil Laverna.

Laverna had always been jealous of her kind twin sister, the Enchantress. In anger she'd released a sickness into the air that killed the plants and took away the fairies'

power to fly. That left only the wingless Elina with the ability to travel to Laverna's lair.

At the time, Elina had no idea what kind of ugliness might be hiding in the lair. Still, she and her pet puffball, Bibble, were willing to go there and fight for Fairytopia! During their travels, Elina and Bibble received help from new friends, like Nalu the merman prince. But in the end, Elina had to face Laverna on her own. Using her brains and courage, brave Elina was able to beat the powerful evil fairy. And for that she had received her wings.

Now Elina could fly just like every other fairy in Fairytopia. But deep down, Elina knew she wasn't like every other fairy. The rainbows that shimmered in her eyes were proof Elina was meant to do great things someday.

But for now, Elina was happy to be able to race in the sky against her best friend, Dandelion. Winning the race was just an added bonus.

"Amazing," Dandelion congratulated Elina on her speed. "You've had your wings for, what, a couple of months? And you're already beating me."

"I know," Elina admitted. "It's weird, isn't it? It's almost like I've had them forever." She twirled in the air. "It's the most incredible feeling."

Bam. Bibble came zooming over to her from behind. He smashed right into Elina's back, sending them both toppling to the ground.

"What's the matter?" Elina asked the fuzzy blue puffball.

Bibble pointed to a nearby pink leaf. "*Blibble blop*," he said.

"You think a pink leaf has been following you?" Elina glanced over at the leaf. There *was* something very odd about this leaf. It had eyes.

Elina glided slowly toward the pink leaf, then, ever so gently, she tapped it and it opened up to reveal long, silky butterfly wings. Just as Elina had suspected, this was no leaf. Rather, it was a magnificent pink-and-yellow Sea Butterfly.

"*Waaa!*" the Sea Butterfly screamed.

"We're sorry we scared you," Elina apologized to the Sea Butterfly. "But why were you following Bibble?"

"What's a bibble?" the butterfly asked her, curious.

Bibble was quite insulted.

"Oh, the puffball," the Sea Butterfly said. "No. I wasn't following Bibble. I was following you. *If* you're Elina. Are you Elina?"

"Yes," Elina replied. "But —"

"You are!" the Sea Butterfly interrupted. "I thought you were. I said to myself, 'Self, that's Elina.' But then, with so many fairies, I couldn't be sure, and how silly would I feel if

I were to come up to some stranger and say, 'Elina, Nalu's in trouble!' and they wouldn't even know who Nalu is, never mind that he's Prince of the Merpeople, so I just followed you and figured I'd —"

"Nalu's in trouble?" Elina interrupted her.

The butterfly looked at Elina, surprised. "How did you know?" she asked. Then, realizing what she'd just said, she apologized. "I didn't mean to break it to you that way. I wanted to ease into it, not just blurt out that Funguses kidnapped —"

"Nalu's been kidnapped by Funguses?" Elina interrupted again. "But that's impossible. The Funguses are Laverna's henchmen. They only work for her, and she was exiled to the Bogs of the Hinterlands."

"I saw it happen at the Crystal Cove," the butterfly insisted. "I wanted to stop them, but I couldn't. Nalu sent me to find you. He says you're the only one who can help."

"What can I do against Laverna's Funguses?" Elina asked.

"A lot," Dandelion assured her. "You've already defeated Laverna once."

"With *help*," Elina reminded her. "I should talk to Azura or another Guardian Fairy. Or the Enchantress."

"There's no time!" the butterfly insisted. "You have to come to the Crystal Cove and help Nalu. He needs you." She flew close to Elina's face. "Will you do it?"

Elina took a deep breath. How could she refuse? "I will," she replied. "Come on, Bibble," she added.

"*Bleeple, bleep, blip,*" Bibble told her, shaking his head insistently.

"Nalu helped us when we needed him,"

Elina reminded him. "Now we can do the same."

There was no way Bibble could argue with that.

"I'm in, too," Dandelion declared. "I'm coming with you."

"No," Elina said kindly. "It could be dangerous. And we may not be back by dark. I don't want to get you in trouble with your mom."

Dandelion frowned. "I can't just wait here," she insisted. "I want to help."

"You can," Elina told her. "If I'm not back by dusk tomorrow, promise me you'll go to Azura for help."

Dandelion reached out her arms and gave Elina a hug. "I promise. Be careful, okay?" She tickled Bibble's head. "You, too, Bibble."

"We will," Elina assured her as she flew off.

Bibble, however, was not so sure that challenging Laverna — *again* — was such a great idea. He called out to Elina, but she was already in flight.

And where Elina went, Bibble always followed.

Chapter 2
Laverna's Command

Bibble had reason to be nervous about what he and Elina were getting into. Just as Laverna had ordered, Prince Nalu was being held captive on the cliffs of Crystal Cove by her evil henchmen, the Funguses.

"Hey, Fungus," one of the henchmen said to his buddy. "Is it just me, or is there something *fishy* about this guy?"

From the shadows of the cliff wall, another Fungus emerged. He may have been smaller than the other two, but he made up

for it with his loud voice and menacing glare. He wore a huge black medallion around his neck. Clearly, this was the Fungus in charge.

"You won't get away with this, Fungus," Nalu insisted.

"Fungus?" he growled. "*These* buffoons are Funguses. *I* come from a more refined stock. Call me Fungus Maximus. Max if you must. And as for getting away with it, I've *already* gotten away with it."

Suddenly, the black gem in the center of his medallion began to swirl. Max gulped nervously as Laverna's image appeared inside the black stone.

"Do you have the prince?" Laverna bellowed.

"We do, Your Most Eminent of Eminencies," Max replied, snapping to attention. "I know just how to make sure he'll take us to the Immunity Berry. Then all you have to do is eat it —"

"And I'll be invulnerable to all magic: past, present, and future," Laverna interrupted with a sinister grin. "My sister the Enchantress will be powerless over me. Get the berry. NOW!"

As Laverna's face disappeared from the medallion, Max turned his attention to Nalu. "Now let's get down to business, shall we? I want you to take me to the Immunity Berry."

"Never!"

Max pulled out a small bottle of liquid and shot Nalu an evil grin.

"I love it when my captives are difficult. It makes my job so much more fun. You will take us to the Immunity Berry or I will release this into the Crystal Cove. Just one drop chokes every bit of oxygen from water, killing everything."

He uncorked the bottle and spilled just a little of the liquid into a nearby tide pool. The water immediately began to bubble, and turned a murky color. "Oopsie," Max sneered. "Look at that."

"I couldn't help you, even if I wanted to. The berry's underwater," Nalu insisted. He frowned. "Last I looked, Funguses don't have gills."

But Max wasn't about to take no for an answer. "I wonder how long it would take for the poison in Crystal Cove to taint all of Mermaidia," he mused, tilting the bottle of poison once again. "Five minutes? Ten? Certainly not enough time to warn anyone . . . *or save them.*"

Nalu sat quietly for a moment, struggling to find some way out of this horrible dilemma. But there was nothing he could do. He had to save his people. "All right. I'll take you to the berry. There's special seaweed you can eat to make you breathe underwater."

Max motioned for one of the Funguses

to dam the tide pool before the poisoned
water could overflow into Crystal Cove.
"Wise choice," he told Nalu, with an evil
grin.

Chapter 3
A Most Unwilling Partner

Not long after Nalu and his captors left Crystal Cove, Elina, Bibble, and the Sea Butterfly arrived at the cliff. Seeing that Nalu was already gone, Elina went straight to work, searching for clues as to where the prince might have been taken.

Bibble joined her, flying low to the ground, his eyes peeled for any sign of Nalu. He was so busy searching that he failed to notice a large domed shell in front of him.

Bong!

The shell let out a loud melodic sound. Bibble giggled and began banging on the shell, playing it like a drum. That caught the attention of the shell's owner, a friendly turtle, who popped his head out and began moving his head to the beat.

At first, Bibble was scared. His bongo drum was alive! But once the turtle shot Bibble a friendly smile, he knew he didn't need to be frightened. Slowly, Bibble smiled back. The little puffball was always happy to make a new friend.

A sudden splash from the water below caught Elina's attention. She watched as a beautiful mermaid with long, pale blue hair and a lavender tail pulled herself up onto the beach.

"Uh-oh." The Sea Butterfly frowned.

"What?" Elina asked her.

"That's Nori. She's a friend of Nalu's." The Sea Butterfly looked frightened. But Elina couldn't imagine why and flew over to introduce herself.

"Hi. I'm Elina," she said cheerfully. "I'm a friend of Nalu's, too, and —"

"*You're* Elina?" Nori definitely didn't sound friendly. "Huh. I mean you're beautiful and all, but you're not *that* beautiful."

"What?" Elina asked, confused.

"Look, I'm sure Nalu would love to see you, but this is where he and I hang out," Nori told her. "So maybe you should just go back to the Fairy Frontier or wherever you're from —"

"The Magic Meadow," Elina corrected her.

"Whatever," Nori replied with a shrug.

She looked around. "Nalu?" she called out.

"Nalu's not here," Elina told Nori gently. "He's been captured by Laverna's Funguses."

"What? How do you know that?" Nori demanded.

"The Sea Butterfly told me he needed my help."

"Nalu sent for *you*?" Nori asked, shaking her head in disbelief. "If Nalu were in trouble, he'd send for me. I know Mermaidia better than anyone."

"Great," Elina replied. "Then you can help me find him."

"No," Nori insisted firmly. "I'll find Nalu myself. I don't need some fairy

getting in my way."

"*Some* fairy?" Elina echoed her. "But Nalu *asked* me. . . ."

Nori didn't wait around to argue. Instead, she dove into the water and swam off.

Bibble looked at the water and then back at Elina. Elina couldn't follow Nori. She had no gills, and couldn't stay underwater for very long.

"I know we can't breathe underwater," she told Bibble. "But wait!" Elina suddenly remembered that the last time she and Nalu had met, he had shown her a way to stay underwater for a very long time.

"We could if we had the seaweed Nalu gave us, remember? I wish we knew where it grows."

Bibble shrugged. He had no idea where it grew. And he didn't want to find out. He just wanted to go home.

But no sooner did Bibble take flight than the little turtle arrived at Elina's side holding magic seaweed in his mouth.

"Yes! That's it!" Elina exclaimed triumphantly. She ate a little of the dark green vegetable. "Come on, Bibble. Eat up," she urged.

Bibble wrinkled his nose. The seaweed smelled nasty. And if he remembered correctly, it tasted pretty nasty, too.

Bibble sighed. There was no arguing with Elina when she set her mind to something. He gobbled up a few of the slimy green strands.

A few moments later, Elina, Bibble, and their turtle friend found themselves underwater. There, the trio came face-to-face with several magnificent sea creatures.

Everything was fine, until the group

reached a fork in the road. Without Nori to guide her, Elina had no idea which way to turn. Should she go left or right?

But the turtle knew what to do. With a gentle nudge, he pushed Elina toward the right. She smiled at the turtle.

The turtle squeaked and swam into the channel beside Elina, making it clear that she would travel the rest of the way to Mermaidia with her.

In fact, Elina thought happily to herself, it seemed all of the sea creatures were willing to go out of their way to help her find Nalu. Except Nori, that is. And Elina couldn't imagine why.

Chapter 4
Meeting the Merfairies

"Mermaidia," Elina sighed as she emerged from the channel. "It's beautiful."

Bibble nodded in agreement. The underwater city was truly gorgeous, filled with merpeople swimming peacefully through the brightly colored seascapes.

But not all the merpeople were so calm. Nori was very worried. She had arrived in Mermaidia shortly before Elina. She was already seeking the help of three merfairies — small pixie-like creatures who had both tails and wings.

"I need to find Delphine," Nori told a yellow merfairy. "It's about Nalu."

"About your future wedding?" the merfairy teased.

"Cut it out," Nori insisted. "Nalu and I are not getting married. He's a prince, remember? I'm a commoner. It doesn't work that way."

The yellow merfairy rolled her eyes. "Please. Everyone knows you're MFEO."

"MFEO?" Nori asked, confused.

"Made for Each Other!" All three merfairies giggled at once.

Nori rolled her eyes. "This is serious," she insisted. "You have to listen to me."

But the yellow merfairy had lost interest in Nori's concerns. Her eyes had landed on someone far more important to her. "Tutu!" she shouted out, zooming toward her pet turtle.

"Fin Fin!" the pink merfairy squealed with delight, as she hugged her pet dolphin.

Nori scowled as she noticed Elina among the crowd of new arrivals. "I thought I told you to leave Mermaidia alone," she insisted.

"You did," Elina agreed. "I didn't listen."

The yellow merfairy swam past the two

arguing girls and made her way to Bibble. "Aren't you the cutest," she cooed, giving him a big hug. "You need lots of love. And cookies."

"Blip! Blip! Blip!" Bibble exclaimed happily. He loved cookies.

"Shouldn't you be running out of air by now?" Nori asked coldly.

"I can breathe," Elina assured her. "Nalu showed me how to use the seaweed."

Nori's face fell. "I guess he really wanted you to spend time underwater," she said.

"Why are you so against me?" Elina demanded. "I want to save Nalu, same as you."

"I don't want an outsider's help!" Nori insisted. "I know what I need to do and . . ." Nori stopped for a second as an idea popped into her head. Suddenly, a smile crossed her lips. "You're right. I've been silly. It's great that you're here. And I know just what you can do."

"Terrific," Elina replied cautiously. She was still unsure of whether or not to trust Nori, but she was willing to try.

"There's a great oracle in Mermaidia," Nori continued. "Her name is Delphine and she knows everything. I'm sure she can tell us where Nalu is. The problem is, only the merfairies know where to find her, or even what she looks like."

"Okay, let's ask them," Elina suggested.

"I've been trying. But merfairies hate to be serious! You can only pin them down for a meaningful conversation if they invite you in for a snack."

"Great. So we'll get invited inside," Elina said.

"But they only eat abovewater. . . ." Nori began.

Now Elina understood. "So that's why you need me."

"I don't need you," Nori insisted. "I'd have found another way to get the merfairies to talk . . . eventually. You might not even be able to do it. The merfairies almost never invite people in for a snack."

At just that moment, the yellow merfairy approached the girls. "Can I bring Bibble inside and make him a snack? I gave him all my cookies, but the poor baby's still starving."

A smile formed on Elina's lips. "I think that's a great idea. Would it be okay if I came, too? He might be more comfortable."

"Deal," the yellow merfairy agreed. "If it'll make Bibble happy, it'll make me happy.

Come on up!"

As Elina swam off behind Bibble and the merfairy, she gave Nori a triumphant look. Nori nodded. Even she had to admit that Elina had been a help . . . at least this time.

Chapter 5
The Oracle's Warning

When Elina and Bibble returned to Mermaidia, they found Nori waiting for them. "So?" the blue-haired mermaid demanded impatiently.

Elina wasn't sure what to reply. The merfairy had indeed answered her question, but the response had made no sense.

Still, maybe Nori could figure it out. "The merfairy said, 'You want to find Delphine, it isn't hard to do, talk to the ferry guide and listen well, too. Delphine has a secret, which from you she'll hide. The shell matters not. Best heed what's inside.'"

Nori nodded slowly, trying to make sense of the message. "The ferry guide . . ." she repeated. "I know where that is. The ferry crosses a river all the way at the edge of Mermaidia." Instantly, she turned and began swimming toward the ferry dock.

Nori had lived her entire life underwater. She was a fast swimmer. There was no way Elina and Bibble could keep up with her. At least not underwater.

There was only one thing to do.

Elina burst out of the water, moving her wings and taking flight. As she soared, she kept her eyes on the water, following Nori's every move. Bibble followed behind, huffing and puffing all the way.

Nori and Elina reached the ferry dock at the exact same time.

"Nice flying," Nori noted.

"Nice swimming," Elina countered. "You weren't trying to ditch me, right?"

"Me?" Nori replied, trying to sound innocent. "Of course not."

Elina looked out onto the water and pointed to a giant snail pulling a raft. "That must be the ferry guide!" she announced.

At that moment, the snail pulled her raft up to the dock. "Three to go across?" she asked.

Nori shook her head. "No. We want to know about Delphine."

"None to go across?" the snail replied. She turned and began to swim away. "All righty, then."

"Three to go across!" Elina called to the snail, in a much kinder tone.

"Why didn't you say so?" she replied, turning back. "Hop on."

As soon as they were aboard the ferry, Nori began questioning the snail. "The merfairies told us you know where Delphine is," she insisted. "So give it up."

The snail frowned. "Sounds like someone got up on the wrong side of the coral bed this morning."

"I want to know where Delphine is," Nori demanded even more forcefully.

The snail sighed. "So dramatic. You'd think it was a real emergency."

Elina sighed. Obviously Nori wasn't getting anywhere. But the snail *was* hiding something. She could tell.

Suddenly Elina recalled what the merfairy had said. *The shell matters not. Best heed what's inside.* "Excuse me," she asked the snail sweetly. "Would you please open your shell?"

"Of course," she said and dove quietly under the water. Elina, Nori, and Bibble followed her, watching in amazement as the snail's shell folded open from the top, revealing a tiny, beautiful mermaid seated on a magnificent throne.

"That's her!" Nori exclaimed excitedly.

"She's exactly like I imagined her."

"What do you wish to know?" the tiny mermaid asked.

"Where is Nalu?" Elina asked.

The tiny mermaid thought for a moment, and then responded, "A sand crab in the hand is worth two in the shell."

"Excuse me?" Nori asked, confused.

"All's fair in love and pufferfishball," the mermaid added.

Elina frowned. That made no sense at all. Which was strange, because oracles were supposed to be wise. . . .

"Wait, I was wrong," Elina admitted suddenly. "The riddle — *The shell matters not. Best heed what's inside.* — I get it now. This isn't Delphine at all. The snail is."

Elina swam over to the snail and looked in her eyes.

"I believe you're Delphine the Oracle," she told the snail. "Will you help us?"

The snail's face filled with compassion. "Of course I will," she assured Elina. "You're looking for Nalu, is that correct?"

"Yes," Elina replied, relieved to have figured out the riddle and found Delphine. "Do you know where he is?"

"I do. But I won't tell you," the oracle continued in a calm, measured voice. She looked from Elina to Nori. "In order to save Nalu, you two will need to take a journey that will require compromise and selflessness. I don't think you are ready for that."

"Please, Delphine," Elina pleaded. "Can't you tell us anything? We really want to help Nalu. Maybe we're more ready than you think."

"Perhaps you are," Delphine agreed. "Travel to the Depths of Despair and seek out the Mirror of the Mist. In order to succeed, you'll have to rely on one another and you'll have to sacrifice." She studied Elina's two legs. "The Depths of Despair are dangerous. They require a great deal of underwater strength provided by a tail . . . not wings. To get to the Mirror of the Mist and save Nalu, you'll need to give up your wings and trade them for a tail."

"I just got these wings," Elina explained. "I can't give them up."

Nori thought for a moment. "You've been swimming just fine without a tail, am I right?" she reminded Elina.

"Yes, I have," Elina agreed.

"See," Nori told Delphine. "So, thanks and all, but we're good."

Delphine said nothing, but opened her shell once again. The tiny mermaid swam out and placed a string of pearls around Elina's neck.

"You can use these pearls to wish for a tail," Delphine explained. "If you do, the pearls will turn deep blue, then one at a time fade back to white. If you are out of the water when the last pearl becomes white again, you'll regain your wings. If not, you'll be a mermaid forever." And with that, the oracle closed her shell and slowly turned away.

Elina was worried. The last thing she'd ever want to do would be to give up her hard-earned wings. But there was no time to think about that now. She and Nori had to get to the Depths of Despair for a glimpse into the Mirror of the Mist.

Chapter 6
Journey to the Depths of Despair

"It's beautiful . . . and strange," Elina murmured with surprise as she and Nori swam down into the Depths of Despair. It was nothing like she'd expected. It was dark and filled with creepy plants. The current was also very strong.

"You just have to swim a little harder," Nori told Elina. She herself dove down even deeper.

As the fast current swirled around her, Elina found it hard to keep up with such an experienced swimmer. But Nori wasn't about to slow down for her. "I'll handle it myself," she told Elina.

Elina frowned. With Bibble insisting on staying at the edge of the Depths of Despair, she really wanted to keep Nori by her side. "But Delphine said we have to work together," she reminded her.

Nori shook her head. "That's a waste of time. Wait for me by the entrance. I promise I'll tell you what the mirror said."

Elina frowned as the mermaid swam off without her. Nori could be stubborn.

A few moments later, Elina heard a cry coming from down below. It was Nori!

"ELINA! HELP!"

Elina looked down just in time to see a huge plant wrap its thick fronds around Nori's waist.

Without a thought for her own safety, Elina swam toward Nori. But the current was too strong. Her legs couldn't help her now. There was only one thing to do. She gripped one of the pearls around her neck.

"I wish to trade my wings for a tail," she said firmly.

There was a burst of light, and Elina's treasured wings disappeared. So did her legs. In their place was a long pink tail. "What have I done?" Elina cried.

But there was no time for regrets. Elina had to save Nori! Using her powerful mermaid tail, she swam down toward Nori.

Nori stared at Elina's new tail with surprise. "Elina, look at you! You . . ."

"Not now," Elina replied firmly. "We have to get you out of here."

Nori nodded and began struggling wildly. Elina pulled at the plant's tendrils, fighting off the wildly waving branches. Once Nori was free, the girls swam off to safety.

But before they could breathe even a single

sigh of relief, they came upon a new, and frightening, sight — two eyes, gleaming in the darkness.

"Who's there?" the owner of the eyes demanded in a deep, dark voice. Elina and Nori grabbed on to each other for support as they came face-to-face with a huge bright-green fish.

"Nori and Elina," Nori replied, suddenly sounding very timid. "We need to consult the Mirror of the Mist."

"We're looking for Prince Nalu," Elina added. "Can you tell us where he is?"

"No," the fish replied.

The girls' faces fell.

"But this can," the fish continued, blinking her eyes in the direction of a clamshell. The shell opened slowly, revealing a huge mirror inside.

"The Mirror of the Mist," Elina murmured.

"Where is Nalu?" Nori asked the mirror. She was wasting no time.

"Are you sure that's what you want to know?" The fish turned to Nori. "Wouldn't you rather know if your true love loves you in return?"

Then she turned to Elina. "Or if you're truly meant to be a fairy with wings. Are you

sure you want to waste the opportunity on Prince Nalu's location?"

"We're not wasting the opportunity," Elina responded.

"We want to know where Nalu is. There's nothing more important," Nori added.

"Very well." The fish sighed.

An image appeared in the mirror. To Elina's eyes, it appeared as though Nalu was tied up outside in the hot sun.

Nori grew frightened. "They can't keep him there. He'll die."

Elina tried to remain calm. "How do we find him?" she asked the fish.

The fish blew a small, sparkly bubble with a swirling rainbow inside. "A beacon," she explained. "Follow it to start on the right path."

The girls swam, following the bubble

back toward the entrance to the Depths of Despair.

Bibble was glad that they were back safely, but when he saw Elina's tail his little jaw dropped.

"*Buuuurple!*" Bibble couldn't believe his eyes. Elina had a tail!

"It's okay, Bibble. I'll explain later. Come on, we need to follow the bubble."

Elina, Nori, and Bibble followed the shimmering bubble through the dark water to another part of the ocean.

When Elina looked at Nori, there was a beautiful blue pattern on Nori's arm. "Your arm!" Elina exclaimed.

Nori glanced over at Elina. The same pattern appeared on *her* arm, but in pink.

"Yours, too!" Nori exclaimed. "It's the Crest of Courage. Our Legend says if you're strong enough to go to the very bottom of Mermaidia, you'll be decorated with the Crest of Courage." She held out her arm. "And we are!"

The girls were so mesmerized by the Crest of Courage on their arms that they didn't notice Bibble getting closer and closer to the bubble. Suddenly, the puffball reached out and popped the magical bubble.

"It was a magic bubble!" Nori shouted angrily at Bibble. She was obviously worried. She didn't think they would be able to find Nalu without the bubble.

"The fish said the bubble would *start* us on the right path," Elina said, trying to calm Nori. "So now we need to choose, up or down?"

Nori thought for a moment. "You're going to think I'm crazy," she said, "but I'm pretty sure Nalu isn't above the water. It's so bright, but he doesn't look dried out. Not like he would be in the sun."

"But where would it be bright like that if it wasn't above the water?" Elina wondered.

Nori pointed bravely toward the fiery path in the distance. "Through the geysers."

Chapter 7
Nalu Is Found

Elina was frightened to swim through the geysers. But she was determined to free Nalu. And Nori firmly believed that if they made their way through the geysers, they would find the prince. So, after summoning Bibble, and convincing him to come along, Elina nervously followed Nori toward the blazing volcanoes.

"It's hard, but I've done it before," Nori assured Elina as she explained how to swim through the fire. "You just have to watch the eruption patterns. Then time it right so you swim through when they're quiet."

The trio watched as the geysers erupted in a series of wild fires, and then quieted down. As soon as the flames subsided, Nori swam through, twisting and turning through the underwater mountains at top speed. When she safely reached the other side, she turned and called out to Elina. "Now you."

"Are you crazy?" Elina insisted. "I can't swim that fast."

"Sure you can. You have a tail now. Use it. Do you trust me?" Nori asked.

Elina thought for a moment. She did trust Nori. So, with Bibble in her arms, Elina took off through the row of geysers. She darted in and out among them, twirling from time to time to keep from being burned. Finally, she made it to the other side.

"You did it!" Nori greeted her excitedly with a hug. "You were amazing! Come on!" She turned and began to swim.

"Look at all the berries!" Elina exclaimed as Nori led them into an underwater cavern that was lined with brightly colored bushes. "Are they edible?"

"Sort of," Nori replied. "Most of them have magical powers." She pointed to the berry bush on her left. "Eat that and you can only talk backwards." She pointed to the bush Bibble was now picking berries from. "That one makes all your hair fall out."

Bibble dropped that berry fast!

Elina swam over toward a group of large golden berries. "What about those?"

"Aren't they beautiful? If you eat one of

those berries it reveals your true self."

Elina grinned. "Are there any love potion berries?" she teased. "You could give one to Nalu."

Nori frowned. "What?" she asked.

"You're in love with him, aren't you?" Elina asked her kindly.

Nori shrugged. "It doesn't matter. Princes don't go for commoners like me."

As the girls spoke, Bibble noticed a bush that appeared to be covered with gumdrop berries. He popped one in his mouth.

"Bibble!" Elina shouted a warning. But it was too late. He'd already eaten the berry. "Please tell me they're not poisonous."

"They're not," Nori began. "They're just . . ."

Bibble opened his mouth to speak. But instead of his usual tone, his voice came out slow and mellow.

"Elina, what's happening? I sound . . . funky." The puffball sounded scared at first, but after a moment he realized how cool this was.

"Well, hello, berry," he said, trying out his new voice. "Don't you look lovely today?"

Nori didn't have time to watch Bibble talk to berries. She and Elina had a job to do. "This way," she said, pointing to a nearby cave.

The trio swam along the corridor until they came to a rock shelf. They pulled themselves up onto the shelf and looked around. Sure enough, they spotted Nalu. He was tied tightly to a steep rock just above the water. Two Funguses were guarding him.

"We have to get him out of there," Nori whispered to Elina.

"I know," Elina agreed. "But how do we distract the Funguses?"

Bibble had an idea. He began to sing. His low, slow, mellow tones were music to the Funguses' ears.

"Snappy," one of the Funguses complimented him.

Bibble flew off into the distance, singing as he moved. The Funguses had to hear more. They followed Bibble as he sang and swam—leaving Nalu unguarded. As soon as they were gone, Nori and Elina pulled themselves out of the water so they could sit beside the prince.

"Nori," Nalu sighed gratefully as she sidled up to him. Then he turned his attention to Elina's tail. "You're a mermaid. What happened?" he asked her.

Elina frowned slightly, recalling her lost wings. She looked down at her pearl necklace. It was almost completely white. "It's a long story," she whispered sadly.

"I don't understand," Nalu said.

"You will," Nori assured him. "But we need to get you out of here before the Funguses come back."

"I can't leave," Nalu insisted. "I told a Fungus where to find the Immunity Berry. The Funguses want to give it to Laverna."

Nori stared at him in amazement. "How could you tell the Funguses where it is?"

"I had to!" Nalu defended himself. "Their leader was going to pour poison in the water. My only hope was to stall and let him get the berry, then make sure he didn't leave with it."

"Sounds good," Nori complimented the prince. "What's the plan for that?"

Nalu blushed sheepishly. "I haven't really figured that out yet," he admitted as Nori and Elina untied his ropes and set him free.

A moment later, Max returned to the ledge, the bright gold and red Immunity Berry in his hands. He was very happy, until he discovered that his prisoner was no longer tied to the cliff. "FUNGUSES!" he bellowed furiously.

Instantly the two foolish henchmen arrived by his side.

"Yeah, boss?"

"Where is the prince?" Max demanded. The two guards looked around. They were shocked to see that in their absence, Prince Nalu had managed to escape.

"Find him!" Max demanded. "If he gets away, he can warn the Enchantress before Laverna eats the berry!"

The mention of Laverna's name was all it took for the Funguses to forget all about Bibble and his singing. That left the puffball free to help Elina, Nori, and Nalu.

"Bibble," Elina called out, poking her head up out of the water, "see that berry the Fungus is holding? I need you to get it."

"*Blip. Bloop.*" Bibble frowned. His funky voice was gone. Even though the effect of the berry had worn off, Elina could still count on him.

As his Funguses searched for Nalu, Max slowly navigated his way down the side of the cliff, taking care not to drop the

Immunity Berry. "Incompetent fools!" he bellowed. "Honestly, how hard is it to watch a fish out of water?"

Just then, Nalu made a spectacular leap out of the water. "Looking for something, Maxie?" he called out.

"Nalu!" Max exclaimed. In his excitement, Max lost his footing. As he struggled to catch his balance, Bibble

appeared as if out of nowhere and grabbed the Immunity Berry from Max's hands.

"Funguses!" Max called out to Laverna's henchmen. "Forget Nalu! Grab the berry!"

Instantly, the Funguses switched their attention to Bibble. They swatted at him, trying to knock him to the ground.

Bibble ducked the rocks and remained unharmed. But he was angry. Without thinking, he threw something at the Funguses. Unfortunately, what he threw was the Immunity Berry!

The two Funguses leaped up and tried to grab it, but Nori burst out of the water, caught the berry, and swam off with it in her arms.

"Get the berry!" Max shouted to the Funguses. Instantly, the Funguses leaped into the water. Bibble followed close behind, determined to be there if Elina needed him.

The struggle for the berry was in full force. Nalu spotted the Funguses leaping toward Nori.

"Nori! Over here," the prince shouted. Nori tossed the berry straight for him, but one of the Funguses caught it instead. Bibble zoomed in and tried to make the Funguses let go.

As Bibble and Nalu fought with the Funguses for control of the berry, Elina called Nori over to her. "I have an idea," Elina whispered to the mermaid. She pointed to the bush with the big golden berries on it.

Nori smiled. She knew exactly what Elina had in mind.

Chapter 8
Elina's Choice

By the time Elina and Nori returned, the game of berry keep-away had left the Immunity Berry in Nalu's hands. But the Funguses were closing in on him.

"Nalu! Throw it here!" Elina called out. Nalu tossed the berry in her direction, and Elina caught it easily. She swam off through a grove of sea plants, with the Funguses close on her tail. Elina tossed the berry to Nori. The Funguses tried to block Nori's hands, but they didn't succeed. Instead, they banged into one another and got tangled up in their own arms and legs.

Suddenly Elina felt something strange going on all around her. She looked down and noticed that there was only a small sliver of blue left on her necklace. She remembered Delphine's warning: *If you are out of the water when the last pearl becomes white again, you'll regain your wings. If not, you'll be a mermaid forever.*

"Nori, now!" Elina shouted.

Nori turned and passed the berry to Elina. In an instant, Elina rushed to the surface and leaped from the water at top speed. A shimmery cocoon formed around her in the air. As Elina's tail began to fade, her wings and legs began to return. "I did it!" she exclaimed.

"So you did," Max agreed, as he joined

Elina on a cliff above the sea. She was still shimmering. Her transformation was not yet complete.

"And now you have a choice. You can give me the berry, or I'll drop this vial of poison in the water. Mermaidia will die out by day's end."

Elina was horrified. She really didn't want to give the Immunity Berry to Max. And yet, she had no choice but to hand over the berry she was carrying.

"How touching," Max sneered as he took the berry from her hands. "You chose to save the merpeople. Too bad they won't live to appreciate it. . . ."

"No!" Elina shouted as Max dropped the vial of poison off the cliff. Without thinking, Elina took a magnificent swan dive off the side of the cliff. She reached out and grabbed the vial of poison, just before it could hit the water.

Elina dove beneath the surface of the water, with the vial tucked safely in her arms. At that very moment, the last bit of blue left her pearls. There was a bright flash and the shimmering cocoon that surrounded Elina burst. Elina had not yet regained her wings and legs when she hit the water. Now she would be a mermaid forever.

Nori, Nalu, and Bibble were as stunned as Elina. They swam toward her and stared at her tail.

"I had to get the vial," Elina explained. A tear fell from her rainbow eyes.

"I can't believe you gave up your wings to save us," Nori said, thanking her.

"I just wish it didn't have to be in vain,"

Nalu added, with a sigh. "The Funguses got away with the berry. Soon we'll all be at the mercy of Laverna."

"That's not true," Nori said, shaking her head. "Elina and I switched the berries. Elina remembered the berry that reveals your true identity and looks really close to the Immunity Berry. That's the berry the Funguses have."

Bibble swam off and rescued the true Immunity Berry from the seaweed patch.

"Then you really did save us," Nalu told Elina gently.

Elina blinked away more tears. She was glad she could help, but the sorrow she felt was unbearable. She would never be able to return to the Magic Meadow.

"This is crazy!" Nori insisted. "There has to be something you can do to get back your wings. You're a fairy. You have wings. You have to fight for them."

Elina shook her head. "I had a feeling everything was too good to last."

Nalu shook his head defiantly. "Elina, I met you before you got that gift. But even then you had wings. You've always flown inside. You have to believe that's who you are. . . ."

Elina looked down at her tail and sighed. "I wish I could."

Nori plucked a single golden berry and handed it to Elina.

"The berry that reveals your true self," Elina said. "Like the one we slipped the Funguses."

"Exactly." Nori smiled. "I believe your true self hasn't changed from the time we met until now. And if I'm right . . . ?"

"Then this berry should turn me into —"

"Your true self," Nori finished Elina's thought. "And no matter what happens, you'll be you: smart and brave and everything that makes you special. To have all that and not have wings, would that be so horrible?"

Elina thought for a moment. "Yeah, it would. It would be really hard. But you're right. I'd still be me, so I'd find a way to be okay."

Elina bravely bit into the berry. The water around her began to churn wildly, spinning Elina around and around. And then she felt something wriggling on her back. Elina gasped. *Her wings!*

"They're different. Look!" Nori pointed out.

Elina glanced over her shoulder. The

wings were huge, and they shimmered. "They are beautiful," Elina said with amazement.

Nalu took Nori by the hand. "Looks like everything turned out perfectly," he said, drawing her close.

Elina smiled, glad that Nori now knew for sure how much Nalu loved her.

"There's only one thing that could make this day better." Elina smirked. "I'd love to be a fly on the wall when Laverna eats that berry."

Nori giggled. She couldn't imagine what Laverna's real self must look like. . . .

~ ~ ~

"The Immunity Berry, Your Wickedness," said Max as he humbly backed away from Laverna.

"Remember this moment, Max, as you watch me come into my destiny!" Laverna took a bite and waited for it to take effect.

However, instead of making her immune to magic, this berry turned her into a toad!

"You fool!" she shouted, as she hopped over to the bog where Max was standing.

"You gave me the wrong berry!" Laverna
looked down at her reflection in the water.
"I'll get you, Elina," she croaked, "if it's the
last thing I do!"

Chapter 9
Taking Flight

Elina felt nothing but happiness as she flew back toward the Magic Meadow.

Meanwhile, Dandelion was in the Magic Meadow waiting for Elina. She had no idea that her best friend was on her way home. She was afraid something dreadful had happened to her.

As she scanned the skies for any sign of Elina, a beautiful voice spoke from behind her. "Don't worry, she's fine."

Dandelion quickly spun around. Her eyes opened wide as she discovered Azura, the beautiful Guardian Fairy.

"But I haven't come to get you yet!" Dandelion exclaimed, recalling the directions Elina had given her before she'd left the Magic Meadow.

"You didn't need to," Azura assured her. She pointed to the sky.

"Elina!" Dandelion gasped from the ground below as she caught sight of her friend's beautiful wings. "Your wings!"

As soon as she spotted Azura, Elina landed on the ground. "You already got her?" she asked Dandelion.

"I came on my own," Azura said. "I wanted to congratulate you on a job well done. I'm very proud of you, you know." She turned and smiled at Bibble. "I'm very proud of you, too," she assured the puffball.

Azura would have loved to have spent

more time with Elina, but she had things to do. As she flew off, she smiled at Elina. "I'll see you again soon, my dear. I promise," she vowed.

Moments later, she was gone, leaving Elina, Bibble, and Dandelion alone.

"Dandelion, you'll never believe it," Elina said as she landed. "It was the most incredible adventure. I don't know where to start."

But Bibble sure did. He was eager to tell Dandelion how he personally saved Mermaidia.

As Bibble jabbered on, Elina glanced at her beautiful wings. They were a symbol of her bravery and sacrifice. Elina knew she would never forget her new friend Nori and all that they had done to save Mermaidia. In fact, every time she caught a glimpse of the magnificent Crest of Courage on her wings, she was certain to remember it all.